INTO THE FIELD GUIDE

A Walk on the Beach

By Laurie Goldman

downtown bookworks

ABOUT THE AUTHOR

Laurie Goldman is a science writer with a passion for the ocean. For many years, she was part of a research team studying the endangered great whales of the western Atlantic. She has also led whale watching cruises out of Provincetown, Massachusetts. She holds a Master's degree in science and environmental journalism and is the author of *Our Changing Climate: The Oceans and Earth's Precious Resources: Clean Energy*. Laurie lives on Cape Cod with her husband and two children.

AUTHOR'S ACKNOWLEDGMENTS

There are many special people to whom I am extremely indebted for help in the preparation of this book. The biggest of thanks to Aija Briga, Fred Dunford, Jody Melander, and Irene Seipt, for generously sharing with me the wealth of their extraordinary seashore wisdom. I also offer my deepest appreciation to the Cape Cod National Seashore, the Peaked Hill Trust, and the Provincetown Center for Coastal Studies, for all that I've learned and experienced over the years from these three invaluable institutions. Thanks to Emily Laber-Warren for her enthusiastic support throughout this project. And finally, a great big hug to my family—Sander, Thea and Liam—for all the wonderful discoveries we've shared exploring our special beaches together.

To my special tribe of friends and family, the Tortilla Flats Yacht Club. You are the folks with whom I first shared the indelible magic of the seashore. My love of the beach and the ocean is forever tied to my love for you all.

downtown bookworks

INTO THE FIELD GUIDE series

Copyright 2013 Downtown Bookworks Inc.

All rights reserved.

Design by Georgia Rucker

Printed in China, January 2013

ISBN 978-1-935703-27-3

10 9 8 7 6 5 4 3 2 1

Downtown Bookworks Inc.
285 West Broadway
New York, NY 10013
www.dtbwpub.com

Contents

Welcome to the Beach

A day at the beach is always an adventure, filled with the sounds of seagulls, the scent of salt, and the crunch of

soft sand underfoot. Many of the animals and plants you see at the beach aren't found anywhere else. A lot of them are pretty. Others might seem a little scary! And there are some things at the seashore that are just plain weird! You may pick up an object and wonder: Is this a plant, an animal, or a rock?

A beach in Florida

From the boulder-tossed shores of Oregon and Northern California to the wide, sandy beaches of Maryland and North Carolina, there are wonderful beaches all over the country. And each one has its own personality. There are the serene, shell-studded shores of the Gulf Coast; the gleaming white sands of Florida's beaches; and the rocky cliffs of Maine. Though every beach is different, they are all similar in one important way. Every seashore is a special meeting place between two worlds—land and sea.

A beach in Maine

A Walk on the Beach will help you to be a keen observer. When you go to the beach, notice the different shapes, sizes, and colors of the shells all around you. Take a close look at the birds that are diving, circling, or hopping along the shore. What's crawling around at the water's edge? There are cool, beautiful treasures all around you. Read on to learn what these treasures are called and what they're doing at the beach.

Each wave that moves up the beach may leave behind something new.

5

Beachcombing

There is a special word for someone who hunts for treasures on the beach: a beachcomber.

Sand dollar

BE PATIENT—AND CURIOUS

When you're beachcombing, look all over. Peer into the water, scan the sand, and even study the sky. Some things will be easy to find. Other interesting critters may be a little trickier to see. An animal may be burrowed in the wet sand or tucked inside a rocky nook. Or it may be tiny and clinging to a dried piece of seaweed. Have patience and take your time exploring.

Bladder wrack

MIND YOUR MANNERS

You want to find neat-looking shells and observe animals you've never seen before. But be careful. You don't want to hurt anything. Many of the living creatures you find on the beach are **marine animals.** That means they live in the ocean. Without the cool salty water of the sea all around them, marine animals will die.

If you pick up an animal for a closer look, be sure you put it back in the same place. That is especially true for animals living in water, but it goes even for the little crabs and snails you might find on the sand and rocks. There is probably a very good reason why that animal chose that special spot as its home.

TAKE A LITTLE, LEAVE A LOT

Many empty shells become cozy homes for other seashore critters. Just about every natural thing on the beach gets recycled one way or another. Instead of taking home all the cool shells you find, pick out a few favorites and leave the rest behind. Make sure there's nothing living in the shells you take. And, of course, never kill a sea creature for its shell.

Hermit crab

You may find a shell with a bit of dead animal inside. It is okay to take this, but if you don't clean it out, it may start to smell. When you get home, have a grown-up help you heat up a pot of water until it is simmering. Put your shells in the pot for a few minutes. You can also leave your seaside treasures outside for a few days until they are completely bleached dry by the sun.

TALKIN' TRASH

There is one thing that you can find on every beach, in every part of the world: TRASH! We all know garbage stinks in more ways than one. Garbage can hurt and even kill sea animals. Sea turtles choke on plastic bags and balloons that they mistake for food. Birds and seals get entangled in old nets and soda-can rings. Take along an extra bag to collect garbage during your beachcombing adventures. You could save a life or two. Just don't pick up anything that looks like it could cut your hands or hurt you.

Rocks, Sand, and Driftwood

Whether you're on a calm, protected inlet, a barrier island, a rocky coast, or a white-sand cove, you will certainly find sand, stones, or washed-up treasures to inspect and explore.

Rock Out!

You will find pebbles of every size, shape, and color at the beach. Smoothed by the waves, beach rocks feel good in your hands. Here are some of the most common, easy-to-identify stones.

Quartz

Quartz is a mineral. Tiny bits of quartz make up the largest part of sand on most beaches around the world. Quartz pebbles are usually white, gray, almost clear, or yellowish.

Agate, a kind of quartz, is rarer—a prized beach find. It is usually gray, white, or brown, but can also be colored, and has cool wavy lines or bands.

Agate

Granite

Granite

Granite varies in color from pink to gray and is speckled with quartz and other minerals.

Basalt

Basalt can be a billion years old! You may see big, gray boulders or smaller stones that have broken off of them.

MEMORY JAR

MAKE IT

The rocks you find at the beach may look shiny and smooth when they are wet. When they dry, they may look a little duller but still be beautiful. Store them in a clear covered jar filled with water to keep their vivid fresh-from-the-ocean look!

SKIP, SKIP, SKIP TO MY LOU

Skipping stones is a lot of fun. Here's how you do it. The perfect skipping stone is flat and about two or three inches wide. A rock that is too heavy or round just won't hop. Hold the rock between the thumb and pointer finger of your throwing hand, keeping it parallel to the water. Keep the stone in that position as you flick your wrist forward and fling it out at the water. The motion is similar to a sidearm Frisbee throw.

Skipping Stones

Sand, Sand Everywhere

What do you *always* bring back with you from a day at the beach? Need a hint? You often carry it home between your toes. That's right: SAND! But what exactly is sand?

SAND FROM ROCKS

If you have a magnifier, take a closer look at a pinch of sand. What do you see? Tiny little rocks. That's what sand is: tiny bits of rocks and minerals that have been on a long, strange trip—a trip that isn't over yet.

A waterfall in Oregon

Far away from the ocean, rocks break off of mountains, then roll downhill into rivers. As they travel in rushing waters, they tumble and bump along riverbeds. Little by little, rocks wear down. The rocks break into smaller and smaller pieces: into pebbles, then gravel, and then the tiny particles we call sand. The gravel and sand are carried by rivers to the sea. And once the sand reaches the ocean, it is carried away by the waves.

FIELD FACT The grains of sand you find might be from rocks that are more than a million years old!

SAND FROM SHELLS

Not all sand comes from rocks. On the beaches of southeast Florida and the Florida Keys, much of the sand is made of crushed shells and the hard parts of marine organisms. The bright white beaches of southwest Florida are made primarily from quartz. Quartz sand is fine and feels soft on your feet.

SAND COLORS

Look at sand under a magnifier. You may see many different colors. That's because sand can be made of many different kinds of rocks and minerals. Tan and white sand is made of quartz, the most common mineral on the planet. Red sand might be bits of the gemstone garnet. Some black sand is made of the mineral magnetite. The black sand of Hawaii is cooled, crushed lava from volcanoes.

FIELD FACT Bring a magnet to the beach and hold it above the sand. It will pick up the black magnetite grains from the rest of the sand.

Tides and Wind

Every year, every day—even every minute—the beach is changing. Have you ever built a sand castle near the water's edge? Did the water inch away from your castle? Or did it get closer and closer, until the whole castle was washed away?

WATCH THE WATER MOVE

The movement of the ocean up and down the beach is known as the **tide.** Believe it or not, tides are caused by the moon! The moon's gravity is pulling everything on Earth toward the moon (just as Earth's gravity pulls everything on Earth toward its center—keeping our feet on the ground). The moon is a lot smaller than Earth, so its gravitational pull is not strong enough for us to notice on land. But it makes a big difference in the ocean. The water responds to the pull from the moon, causing the tides we see every day.

High tide is when the water moves to its highest point on the beach. **Low tide** occurs when the water has fallen all the way back out. In most places, there are two high tides and two low tides every day.

FIELD FACT Some areas around the Gulf of Mexico have only one high tide and one low tide a day. This phenomenon is called a diurnal tide.

14

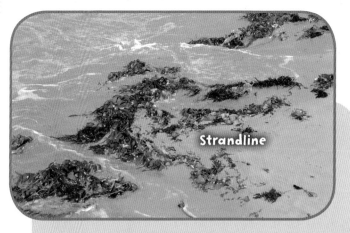
Strandline

STROLLING THE STRANDLINE

Low tide is the best time for beachcombing because you can see many plants, animals, rocks, and shells that are hidden underwater during high tide. Look for a line of dried seaweed along the beach that runs parallel to the waves. It's called the **strandline.** That's how far the water reached during the last high tide. Walk between the strandline and the water, and you'll find a lot of cool stuff.

THE POWER OF WIND

Tides aren't the only things changing the beach. Wind changes seashores too. Even if you build your sand castle high up on the beach, far away from the waves, it will disappear. Grain by grain, the dry sand of your sculpture will eventually blow away.

Winds push the water around too. Windy storms can make big, strong waves that can alter a beach in just a few hours. The surf drags sand from one shore and spits it out somewhere else.

FIELD FACT Use a magnifier to examine some sand. In general, you will find larger grains of sand on beaches with stronger waves. That's because very fine sand is more likely to be carried away in the surf.

Flotsam and Jetsam

Flotsam was a term once used to describe the floating remains of a shipwreck, but now it refers to any object found floating in the water. *Jetsam* refers to things that have been cast overboard to lighten a ship's load.

Driftwood

Driftwood

LOOK WHAT WASHED ASHORE

Keep an eye out for twisted pieces of driftwood, colorful pieces of sea glass, and dollops of seafoam. **Driftwood** is most often the remains of branches or trees that have been washed into the ocean and made smooth by the waves. You might notice holes and patterns in driftwood. These "designs"

Shipworm holes in a piece of driftwood

were made by little animals like the shipworm or gribble, which spend their entire lives burrowing into pieces of waterlogged wood.

Sea glass

Sea glass was once part of an empty bottle—perhaps lost in a shipwreck or storm, though more likely dropped in the water or on the beach by a thoughtless person. The powerful forces of the waves and sand polish the sharp ends of glass shards until they are smooth and frosty. Clear, brown, and green sea glass are most common. The rarest finds are blue, red, and orange. With fewer glass bottles being used now, sea glass is a great collectible.

Seafoam forms when there is a lot of seaweed offshore. The churning water breaks down the plants, which act as foaming agents. Seafoam can make the water look like a giant bubble bath.

Seafoam

Animals

In this chapter, you will learn about
the crabs scurrying in the sand,
the birds soaring overhead,
the clams you know best by the shells
they leave behind, and other animals
that live at the water's edge.
Look up, down, and all around you—
even underneath the sand and in
the water. Watch these creatures
move. See what they eat, how they
hide, and where they hang out.

Shells as Living Things

Shells are different from rocks and sand in many ways, but one difference really stands out. Every shell you find was once part of a living animal.

SKELETONS

We have our skeletons inside our bodies, but lots of animals have their skeletons on the outside. These hard outer coverings, called exoskeletons, help protect and support these animals' soft bodies. Most shells are the exoskeletons of mollusks (see page 22). Not all mollusks have shells. Slugs, squid, and octopuses are mollusks that do not have shells.

While they are alive, shelled creatures look very different from the empty shells you may find on the beach.

Live Sea urchin

For example, when it is alive, a **sea urchin** is covered with sharp spikes. When it dies, the spines fall out. All that is left is a hollow ball-shaped shell called a test.

Sea-urchin tests

Live scallop

A **scallop** also looks completely different when it's alive and in the water. It is a busy creature with eyes along the open side of its shell.

Scallop shell

Scallop eyes

FIELD FACT Scallop eyes might be blue, red, or gold. The scallop's eyes aren't very advanced. They can't make out shapes, but they can see light and movement.

ANIMALS

HOME, SWEET HOME

Shells serve as homes and protection for many animals found in and around the water. If it is too hot, too cold, or too dry, or if there is a scary predator nearby, a mollusk can shut itself up tight inside its sturdy shell. Mollusk shells come in all shapes and sizes. They can look plain or have intricate patterns or bright colors.

The Wide World of Mollusks

Most of the shells you find on the beach come from a huge group of animals called mollusks. Mollusks are a group of soft-bodied animals that include clams, mussels, snails, conchs, oysters, and limpets. Many kinds of mollusks live in the shallower parts of the sea and at the seashore.

TWO HALVES MAKE A WHOLE

Scientists have divided mollusks into categories based on characteristics such as how their shells are built. One group of mollusks you are sure to see at the beach is the bivalves. (*Valve* means "shell," and *bi* means "two.") These are animals that have two hard shells hinged together in the middle. These animals live in the same shell their entire life. The shells grow as the bivalve grows. When a bivalve dies, its soft body parts decay. The shell is all that's left. Eventually, the material that holds the two shells together also decays, and the shells separate. That's why you will often find single bivalve shells on the beach. But you may find two shells still attached.

FIELD FACT You can get an idea of how old a bivalve is by counting the ridges on the top of the shell. They are like the growth rings of a tree.

Ridges on a clamshell

COMMON BIVALVES

The **quahog** (*ko*-hog) clam is also known as a littleneck, cherrystone, or hard-shell clam. Parts of the inside of the shell are often purple. (For more on clams, see pages 24–25.)

Quahog

Mussels anchor themselves to rocks with strong threads. When they want to move, they just let go of the thread and move to a better spot. They can move as much as a foot a day. (For more on mussels, see page 29.)

Mussel

The **scallop** has a fanlike, ribbed shell. Scallops are good swimmers. If a scallop feels threatened, it can really move! It travels by snapping its shell shut again and again, each time shooting out a spurt of water that pushes it along.

Scallop shell

ANIMALS

THAT'LL BE 10 SHELLS, PLEASE

Some Native Americans used shell beads, or wampum, to commemorate important events. When European settlers realized how important the beads were, they began to manufacture them and use wampum as currency. Native Americans used the white spiral part of whelks (see page 36) and the purple part of quahogs to make their beads.

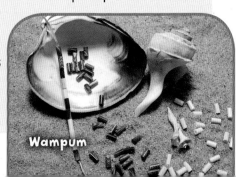
Wampum

Clams

Like all bivalves, clams have two shells connected in the middle, but there is a lot of variety in their sizes and shapes.

SUPER DIGGERS

At low tide, you may see an **Atlantic jackknife clam** lying motionless on the wet sand. But if you reach down to pick it up, it may disappear in a flash! The jackknife clam escapes by burrowing into the sand, tunneling faster than you could possibly dig after it. These animals are also called razor clams because they are shaped like old-fashioned straight-edged razors.

Live Atlantic jackknife clam

Atlantic jackknife clamshell

Pacific razor clams, found on the West Coast, are wider than Atlantic jackknife clams.

Live Pacific razor clams

Pacific razor clamshell

PEEK-A-BOO

Many kinds of bivalves burrow under the sand during low tide. Look for round holes in the wet sand. Each hole might just be a different creature's hideout! If you have a shovel, carefully dig into the sand and see what small animals you can uncover. Just look—don't touch—and leave them where you found them.

CLAMS COME IN MANY SIZES

The **surfclam** is the biggest bivalve found on U.S. shores. The largest one ever recorded was 8.9 inches long (though it is rare for these clams to grow larger than 8 inches). Found along the East Coast from Maine to North Carolina, these clams are often used to make clam chowder.

Surfclam

FIELD FACT The largest bivalve in the world is the deep-sea giant clam, or *Tridacna gigas*. Its shell is nearly four feet across, and it can weigh as much as 600 pounds.

Giant clam

Amethyst gem clam shells are found all along the Atlantic and Gulf coasts, and have been introduced to the Pacific as well. Even on beaches where there are thousands of them, you may not see them at first. They're teeny tiny—the largest adults are only as wide as a No. 2 pencil eraser.

Amethyst gem clam

ANIMALS

25

Cockles, Coquinas, Angel Wings, and Ark Shells

Some bivalve shells are easy to recognize because of their distinct shape.

Giant Atlantic cockle

It's hard to imagine that the **giant Atlantic cockle** can move around without legs or fins, but it does. In fact, some are real acrobats. Cockles escape predators by leaping to safety. Common along the Atlantic coast from North Carolina to Florida, they can grow to be five inches long.

Heart cockle

Heart cockles (also known as basket cockles), found in Alaskan waters and along the Pacific coast, usually aren't more than five inches long. When you hold one sideways, you can see how this critter got its name!

Coquinas are often found on Florida seashores. When these colorful shells are open and flat, some say they look like delicate little butterflies lying in the sand.

Coquinas

Angel wing

Angel wings are white, ribbed shells shaped like (you guessed it!) wings.

The interior of an **ark shell** looks like a tiny, old-fashioned boat. These shells come in many different colors and patterns. **Turkey wings** are a colorful type of ark shell. With their zebra-like stripes, these wing-shaped shells really stand out in the sand.

Ark shell

Ark shells

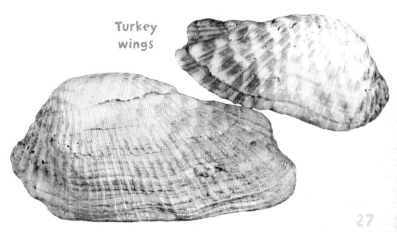

Turkey wings

Oysters, Mussels, and Jingle Shells

Shells can be smooth, bumpy, curved, or flat. Be on the lookout for these eye-catching bivalves.

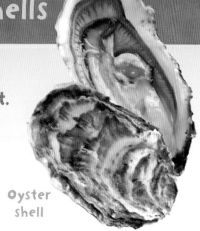

Oyster shell

OYSTERS

Oyster shells are bumpy. There is a reason oysters look so different from other bivalves. After baby oysters are born, they swim around for a few weeks until they find a nice, hard spot to settle down. The oyster will remain there for the rest of its life. As it grows, its shell takes the shape of whatever surface it's attached to.

FIELD FACT Young oysters are called spat.

SEASIDE TREASURES

Oysters are known for the treasures that can grow inside their shells: pearls. These precious jewels start out as grains of sand. The sand gets inside an oyster's shell and irritates the animal. To soothe the irritation, the oyster covers the grain of sand with a smooth substance called mother-of-pearl. The sand is covered with layer after layer of mother-of-pearl for years until finally a beautiful, round pearl is complete. Now, people put sand grains inside oysters on purpose to grow pearls—these are called cultured pearls.

Pearl necklace

MUSSELS

You can often find hundreds of mussels grouped together on a single large rock. They live underwater, but many are uncovered during low tide. They survive being out of the water for short periods by tightly closing up their shells.

A bed of mussels on the coast

FIELD FACT A single mussel can produce 10 million to 20 million eggs in a year.

AMERICAN JINGLE SHELLS

American jingle shells are also known as toenail shells or mermaid's toenails. They are shimmery and almost flat. You can see the light shining through them. Unlike clams and oysters, the bivalves that live inside jingle shells taste bitter, so people do not eat them.

Jingle shells

JINGLE JEWELS

MAKE IT

Many jingle shells already have a hole through them. The bivalve that lives inside a jingle shell makes a fine, strong thread that passes through that hole to anchor the shell to a hard surface, like a rock. Because of the ready-made holes in these pretty shells, they are perfect for craft projects. String a bunch of shells onto a cord or earring wire to make jewelry.

You can also use them to create natural wind chimes. String bunches of jingle shells onto different lengths of string or fishing line. Tie the strings around a piece of driftwood. Tie another piece of fishing line around the center of the driftwood, and use it to hang your wind chime outside your door or in a window.

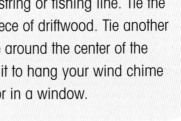

ANIMALS

Meet the Gastropods

There are other kinds of mollusk shells you might find in your beachy adventures. One big group is called the gastropods. *Gastropod* means "stomach foot." When these animals move around, it looks like they are walking on their stomach. Even if you've never been to the beach, you've probably met a gastropod or two, such as a snail.

Snail

FIELD FACT Not all gastropods have shells. A slug is one member of this soft-bodied group of animals that lives without a shell.

Slug

SPIRAL SHELLS

Most gastropods live in a single shell that looks different from the shells of other mollusks. The shell twists around and around itself into a tightly wound spiral. As it grows, the gastropod's soft body also twists to fit snugly inside its curvy shell.

A spiral shell

View inside a spiral shell

Spiral shells vary greatly in shape and color. Here are a few neat spirals you may come across.

The **Atlantic oyster drill shell** is usually yellowish-white or gray, with brown spiral bands. It can be found on both the East and West Coasts of the United States.

Atlantic oyster drill shell

There are hundreds of different kinds of **murex shells,** including the **lace murex** and the **pink-mouthed murex.** These spiney shells are found on shores from North Carolina to Florida and in California and Texas.

Pink-mouthed murex shell

Lace murex shell

FIELD FACT
In ancient times, murex shells were used to make purple dye.

The **common fig shell** is often called a paper fig. The shell is sturdy, but looks like it is paper thin. It usually grows to be three to four inches long.

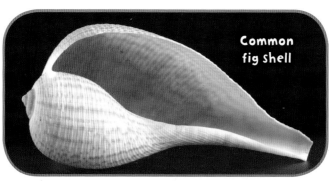

Common fig shell

31

Moon Snails, Turbans, Olives, and Cowries

Some spiral shells are rounder, and others are more egg-shaped.

Moon snails have high, smooth, ball-shaped shells. When a moon snail comes upon a clam or mussel it wants to eat, it climbs on top of its prey and covers it entirely with its fleshy "foot." Then it uses its sawlike tongue (see page 35) to drill a hole through the shell of its victim, and sucks out the soft body of the clam or mussel inside. If you find an empty clamshell with a neat little hole in it, you will know a moon snail has been at work! One common moon snail is the **shark-eye.**

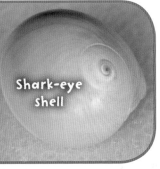

Shark-eye shell

Live shark-eye moon snail

Moon snails lay eggs, and then coat them with sand and mucus, forming a wide, ribbonlike collar. Sometimes, you can find these **sand collars,** or egg collars, washed up on the beach. Even though they are made mostly of sand, they are sort of rubbery and flexible. When they dry out, they will crumble.

Sand collar

Turban snails, like **black turban snails** (common in California), have thick, heavy shells.

Black turban snail shell

Chestnut turban shells, found on the East Coast, have a bumpy surface and do not usually grow larger than half an inch wide.

Chestnut turban shell

Olive shells are oblong and come in different shades—sometimes with patterns. Olive snails are fast burrowers.

Olive shells

The aperture of a cowrie shell

Cowrie shells are tiny, smooth, and egg-shaped, with long, narrow openings. In some parts of the world, cowries were used as currency, and they are used in many places for making jewelry.

FIELD FACT The opening in the shell where the sea creature can move in and out is called an aperture.

Live Atlantic deer cowrie

Atlantic deer cowrie shell

Conchs and Periwinkles

Conchs and periwinkles are two types of spiral-shelled gastropods that people eat.

CONCHS

Conch shells are large and heavy, and their insides are smooth, shiny, and often colorful. Some people say that if you hold a conch shell to your ear, you can hear the ocean roaring inside. The **queen conch** is also known as the pink conch, because of the soft pink color inside the shell.

Live conchs

Queen conch shell

Queen conch's eyes

The **spider conch** has distinct spikes.

FIELD FACT The word *conch* is pronounced "konk."

Spider conch shell

A RAD TONGUE

Gastropod tongues are very different from ours. Even the littlest gastropod has an extra-long tongue called a **radula.** The radula is thin and ribbonlike, and lined with sharp teeth! It is a useful tool to help the gastropod find its food. Depending on the gastropod, the radula can be used as a saw, drill, or grinder. Some even use it as a spear. It's like having a Swiss Army knife for a tongue! Many gastropods are good hunters.

The work of a radula

PERIWINKLES

You can often find **periwinkles** in groups attached to rocks at low tide. Because these tiny snails can shut themselves up tight in their shells, they are able to stay out of water longer than most sea animals.

Periwinkle Shell

A periwinkle will use its radula to scrape seaweed off rocks and even other shellfish. They may be tiny, but their constant scraping can wear down the surface of a rock.

A living periwinkle is only about an inch and a half tall, but its radula can be five inches long! Lined with as many as 3,500 microscopic teeth, the radula stays coiled up in the back of the snail's mouth when the snail isn't feeding.

Live periwinkles

Whelks

Waved whelk

Whelks are another group of gastropods. Unlike conchs and periwinkles, these sea snails are carnivores, which means they eat other animals.

People in many parts of the world like to eat whelks, which are found along the East Coast and in other countries. Whelk shells can look a lot alike, but here are some ways to tell them apart. The shell of a **channeled whelk** is smooth. It has faint stripes of brown on the outside and is orange inside.

Channeled whelk

A **knobbed whelk** is one of the largest whelks. It has a ring of bumps, or knobs, all around the wide part of its shell.

Knobbed whelk

There are many types of **basket whelk shells.** One of them, the small, rounded **dog whelk,** can be found on rocky shores.

Dog whelk

Found in the southeastern U.S., the **lightning whelk** is the official state shell of Texas.

Lightning whelk

SPECIAL DELIVERY!

The egg case of a whelk looks like a bunch of disks attached to a cord. It is curled into a spiral, and often washes up on beaches. At first glance, you might think it is just a piece of garbage. Take a closer look.

The egg case of the channeled whelk looks like a bunch of golden paper coins strung together. You can shake them like a rattle. Ask a grown-up to help you open up one of these disks to find out what makes that jangly sound. If you're lucky, you might find a dozen or more baby shells inside. Each one will look like a tiny copy of its parent.

The egg case of the **waved whelk** looks more like a dried-out ball of Rice Krispies!

Egg case of the channeled whelk

Waved whelk egg case

FIELD FACT

When wet and rubbed against something, waved whelk egg cases give off a bubbly liquid. Many years ago, sailors on long ocean voyages would scrub themselves clean with these egg cases. They were known as "merman's soap."

Limpets

Some animals survive in the rough, churning ocean by hanging on fiercely to anything hard they can find, whether it's a rock, the bottom of a boat, or even another animal!

Limpets

HOLD ON TIGHT!

A **limpet** is a type of gastropod that makes its home in one place for its whole life. But that doesn't mean it stays put forever. At night, it moves around, grazing on seaweed-covered rocks. A strong foot and a cap-shaped shell enables it to do this.

Keyhole limpets have a small hole in the center of the shell.

Keyhole limpet

The outside of the **Atlantic plate limpet** has brown markings or blotches.

Atlantic plate limpet

The **fingered limpet,** or ribbed limpet, is common on the Pacific coast.

Fingered limpet

STACK THEM UP!

Slipper shells look like little slip-on shoes.

Slipper shells, or slipper limpets, definitely won't fit on your feet! Turn them upside down, though, and you will see the little pocket they are named for. Slipper shells usually live on top of one another in little towers. You often find these slipper-shell heaps stuck to rocks or large shells.

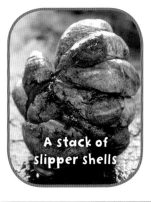

A stack of slipper shells

Slipper shells spend their entire lives like this. The youngest ones are on top. They are always male. The ones at the bottom are the oldest, and they are female. These animals change from male to female as they grow!

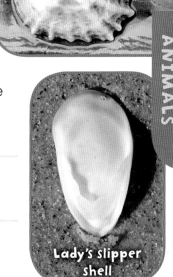

Spiny slipper shell

The **spiny slipper shell** has a rough, bumpy shell.

Lady's slipper shells, or white slipper limpets, are often attached to hermit-crab shells.

Lady's slipper shell

Found on the California coast, the **onyx slipper shell** has an extra-glossy interior. The interior color can vary from tan to very dark.

Onyx slipper shell

Chitons

Chitons (ky-tens) are not bivalves (like clams and oysters) or gastropods (like slugs, snails, and limpets). They are a totally different kind of mollusk, with eight overlapping shell segments, or plates.

UNDERWATER ROLY-POLIES

These creatures are oval and flat. They do not have a head or a foot. Chitons stay put during the day, holding on to rocks and other surfaces. When a chiton becomes detached, it rolls up into a little ball for protection—just like an armadillo.

Chitons wander around all night looking for food. They have a rough, sandpaper-like radula (see page 35) that enables them to scrape algae (see page 100) off rocks. Some species return to the exact same rocky nook when they're done eating.

When a chiton dies, the eight-part shell comes apart. The individual shell plates you find washed up on the shore are shaped like butterflies.

A single chiton shell plate

On the West Coast, you may find the **giant chiton,** also known as the gumboot chiton. It can reach one foot in length.

Giant chiton

Mossy chitons may be overgrown with algae, which makes them hard to spot. The shell is also covered in long, rubbery hairs. This is one of the species that always returns home to the same spot.

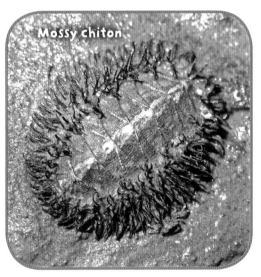

Mossy chiton

Lined chitons range in color from pink to lavender. They are covered in zigzagged lines that are usually red, blue, pink, or white.

Lined chiton

Intro to Crustaceans

Lobsters and crabs have shells, but they aren't mollusks. Their shells are made of many different parts connected together like a knight's suit of armor. Sea animals with this kind of shell are called **crustaceans** (cruh-stay-shunz). Crustaceans come in many shapes and sizes, from tiny, unmoving barnacles to huge, long-legged spider crabs.

FIELD FACT The word *crustacean* is easy to remember if you think about how the hard shell makes the outside of these critters crusty. (Get it? *crust*-y *crust*-aceans).

LOBSTERS

Lobsters are crustaceans, but they live in deep water, so you don't usually see them at the beach. Alive and in the water, most lobsters are dark green or brown. After they've been caught and cooked, their shells turn bright red. If you find a bright-red lobster shell in the sand, look for a bib. It is probably just left over from a beachside clambake.

Live lobster

Cooked lobster

Crab eyes

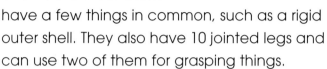

CRABS

There are nearly 5,000 types of **crabs,** with different shapes, sizes, and habits. All of them have a few things in common, such as a rigid outer shell. They also have 10 jointed legs and can use two of them for grasping things.

Many crab's eyes are on long stalks that stick out from its shell. Like a submarine's periscope, they let the crab see in all directions. Many crabs hunt for food by hiding in the sand with only their eyes sticking out. When they see something yummy swimming by, they pounce!

ANIMALS

MOLTING—HOW REVOLTING!

Just like you grow out of your clothes as you get older, crabs and other crustaceans grow out of their shells. When a crab gets too big for the shell it's in, the crab wriggles out of it (just like you might squeeze out of a tight sweatshirt), and makes a new, larger one.

Because they grow so fast, young crabs need to molt every few weeks. Adults might molt only once a year. With no shell to protect it, a crab is in a lot of danger after molting. It takes a few days for the new shell to harden. A male crab often guards over a female with eggs while she is molting.

A crab shell abandoned during molting

Colorful Crabs

From green and blue to pink and tan, crabs come in many different colors.

Female blue crab

The **blue crab** has long, sharp spikes on either side of its shell, making it easy to recognize, but dangerous to handle! Like all crabs, it has five pairs of legs that do different jobs. The front two legs have claws for hunting and protection. Other legs are for walking. On a blue crab, the back two legs have paddles for swimming. Blue crabs are found along the East Coast. Maryland's Chesapeake Bay is home to a large population.

Only the male blue crab has blue claws. The tips of the female's claws are bright red: It looks like she's wearing fingernail polish! It is important to stay away from these critters (both males and females) and their powerful claws.

Dungeness crabs, common on the West Coast, have distinctive marks on their shells. They are usually reddish-brown or purplish with white-tipped claws.

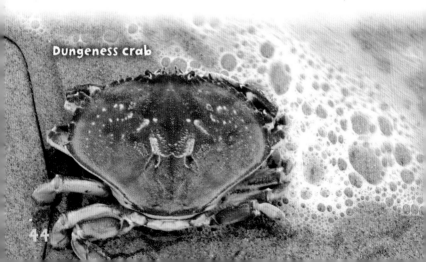

Dungeness crab

Lady crab

Not all **lady crabs** are girls. The shell of the lady crab looks like it's covered with pinkish leopard spots. If you find a live lady crab, be careful! They have strong claws, and could give you a nasty pinch.

FIELD FACT A crab's tail is folded up under its body. The males have narrow tails that sort of look like the Empire State Building. A female's tail is much wider.

The **green crab** is found all over North America— and the world.

Green crab

ANIMALS

The **spider crab** has a round body and long spindly legs—just like a spider.

Spider crab

FIELD FACT The largest spider crab can measure nine feet from claw to claw!

NATURE FINDS

COLLECTOR'S TIP If you find a lifeless crab on the beach and you aren't sure if it is an empty shell that a crab has grown out of, look closely. A straight slit along the back edge of the shell is a sign that the animal moved out of that shell.

Little Crabs

Fiddler crabs and ghost crabs are rarely larger than two inches wide.

Male **fiddler crabs** are easy to spot. They have one oversize claw that is mostly just for show. Female fiddlers' claws are the same size.

Fiddler crabs live in little tunnels in seashore sandbanks and mudflats. It's fun to watch them skittering around at low tide. At first, they might be spooked by you, but if you stay very still, they will go back to their business, popping in and out of their holes and looking for things to eat in the sand. If a male fiddler crab sees a tunnel he likes better than his own, he will try to scare off the crab that lives there. He will wave his big claw and act tough. Males can get into serious wrestling matches.

Male fiddler crab

FIELD FACT Most fiddler crabs are right-handed. If a male's big claw is broken off in an accident or a fight, the smaller left claw will grow to replace it.

Ghost crabs are hard to see. With their yellowish or tan coloring, they blend into the sand.

Ghost crab

Hermit crab

Hermit crabs aren't like other crustaceans: Because their exoskeletons are thin and weak, they need to protect themselves by living in the empty shells of other animals. Like Goldilocks, hermit crabs are always looking for something that fits *juuusssst* right! When the crab outgrows the shell it's in, it moves to a bigger one.

Some hermit crabs like to decorate their new homes. A hermit crab may put a piece of sponge or a sea anemone on top of its shell to help hide from predators.

Hermit crabs often have roommates. Slipper shell limpets like to hitchhike on top of their shells. Some types of underwater worms tuck themselves inside the shell with the hermit crab and feed on the crab's leftovers.

THE SHELL GAME

NATURE FINDS

If you find a hermit crab while you are wading in the water, you can get a closer look at it. Put it in a bucket, magnifying jar, or glass dish filled with a few inches of cool salty water and a layer of sand on the bottom. (Take the water and the sand from somewhere near where you found the hermit crab.) Put several empty shells of various sizes in with the crab. They especially like moon snail shells (see page 32). See whether it tries any of them on for size. When you are done looking, put the crab back exactly where you found it.

Hermit crab

Tiny Crustaceans

Here are two crustacean cousins of crabs: one is an itty-bitty marine scavenger, which means that it will feed on anything it finds, including dead matter. The other spends nearly all of its life inside its shell.

Sand hopper

UP, UP, AND AWAY!

There is an acrobatic critter you can see perform daily in the dried seaweed at the strandline. It's called a **sand hopper,** sea flea, or beach flea. It is less than one inch long, but it can jump 50 times its height! Unlike fleas, these tiny critters are not insects, and they do not bite. Sand hoppers are a kind of crustacean called an amphipod. Use a magnifier to get a closer look. An amphipod's body is unusual. It is flat, as if it's been squeezed between two fingers, which makes it really hard to spot.

FREEZE! DON'T MOVE

As babies, **barnacles** swim around. Then, like limpets or chitons, they attach themselves to any hard underwater surface, such as a rock, shell, dock, or boat.

Barnacles on a scallop shell

There are even some barnacles that live on whales! Once they are attached, they stay put, with their heads down and their feet sticking out of the hole on top. You can find hundreds of them all squeezed together on a large rock.

Gooseneck barnacles have a stalk that resembles a goose's neck and shells that look like a goose's head. **Acorn barnacles** are white or gray and look like tiny volcanoes.

Barnacle goose

Long after a barnacle has died, its empty shell remains. Barnacle shells are usually made up of six pieces. Be careful: Don't walk on barnacles with bare feet. Their shells are very sharp!

Gooseneck barnacles

Acorn barnacles

Scientists study how barnacles attach themselves to rocks. They hope to make underwater glues as sticky and strong as the stuff barnacles make.

FIELD FACT In less than two years, 10 tons of barnacles can attach to a tanker ship.

ANIMALS

FOOT FEEDERS

At low tide, when barnacles are no longer underwater, they shut their shells up tight to keep from drying out. When the tide comes up and they are underwater, the shells open up again. Look closely, and you can see the feathery legs of the barnacles moving around. They are trying to push microscopic animals floating in the water into the shell to be eaten.

Gooseneck barnacles

49

Horseshoe Crabs

Horseshoe crabs have been around for hundreds of millions of years. People call them living fossils because they look the same now as they did when they shared the beach with dinosaurs.

Horseshoe crab

A horseshoe crab has a spiky tail. It may look like a dangerous sword, but it's a tool, not a weapon. When a horseshoe crab gets tossed upside down in the waves, it uses its tail as a lever to right itself.

Horseshoe crabs are not crabs. They are actually related to spiders. If you carefully turn over a living horseshoe crab, you will see that underneath that big helmet-shaped shell, its body looks a lot like its cousin the scorpion.

Horseshoe crab

ABANDONED SHELLS

Just like crustaceans, horseshoe crabs have to shed their shells as they grow. You can often find the empty ones on the beach.

Some are tiny and others quite large. Look for the split along the front of the shell where the animal wriggled out. It takes 10 years for a horseshoe crab to grow to adulthood.

FIELD FACT A horseshoe crab has 10 eyes! You can see two of them on the top of its head. Seven others are on the animal's body, and one is on its tail.

EGG-LAYING RITUAL

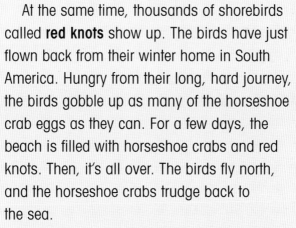
Red knot

There are certain beaches where an amazing ritual occurs every spring. Huge numbers of female horseshoe crabs crawl out of the sea and march up the beach to the highest high-tide line. There, they bury their eggs in the damp sand.

At the same time, thousands of shorebirds called **red knots** show up. The birds have just flown back from their winter home in South America. Hungry from their long, hard journey, the birds gobble up as many of the horseshoe crab eggs as they can. For a few days, the beach is filled with horseshoe crabs and red knots. Then, it's all over. The birds fly north, and the horseshoe crabs trudge back to the sea.

The eggs that remain will stay buried until the next full moon. Then high tide will wash over them, moving the sand and uncovering the newly hatched baby horseshoe crabs. The little ones make their way down the beach and into the ocean.

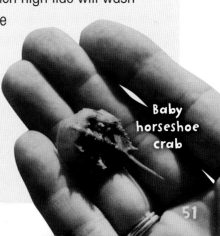
Baby horseshoe crab

Tide-Pool Life

A tide pool in California

Tide pools are rocky holes that stay filled with water even when the tide goes out. They are wonderful to explore. Many plants and animals live in them.

Tide pools show you a snapshot of what life is like under the ocean. They let you sneak a peek at sea creatures going about their daily business. Sea anemones and sculpin are two creatures you might spot in a tide pool.

AN ANIMAL THAT LOOKS LIKE A PLANT

Are there flowers in your tide pool? These are actually animals called **sea anemones** (ah-*nem*-o-neez). They are related to jellyfish. What look like petals are actually the stinging tentacles an anemone uses to catch food. Anemones use their tentacles to paralyze fish and pull them into the mouth hidden underneath. When competing for space, sea anemones will even sting each other. But don't worry, the stingers won't hurt you.

Sea anemones are very sensitive to danger. If you startle one, it will pull its tentacles in and shrink down into a lump. Wait a few moments, and it will open up again.

Sea anemones

Sculpin

HIDING IN PLAIN SIGHT

At first glance, you might not see much going on in a tide pool. That's because many of the animals living there are well hidden. Watch for a while, and you may see the water come to life.

Many sea creatures hide from predators by disguising themselves to look like their surroundings. This sneaky survival tactic is called camouflage. What looks like a rock may be a small armored fish called a **tide-pool sculpin.** Also called tide-pool Johnnies, sculpins take on the color of the tide pool they live in, making them hard to see against a rocky background. Their eyes are on the top of their spiny head, so even if you can't see them, they can see you!

Sculpin

ANIMALS

What Is an Echinoderm?

Sea urchin up close

Sea urchins, sand dollars, sea biscuits, and sea stars belong to the group called echinoderms (ee-*ky*-no-durmz). The word *echinoderm* means "spiky skin."

A **sea urchin's** mouth is under its body, surrounded by tiny tube feet. After a sea urchin

Sea urchin

dies, its spikes fall off. The round, hollow shell left over is called a **test.**

Long-spined sea urchin

Unlike a porcupine, a sea urchin can't shoot its needles at you. A purple or green sea urchin is safe to handle. But don't touch the barbed spines of the **long-spined sea urchin** found in Florida's warm waters. They are very sharp, and can hurt a lot if you bump into them.

FIELD FACT Those spines don't keep everyone away. Many animals, like sea otters, brave them to get to the meat inside. Humans like them too: They are a popular dish in Japan.

NATURE FINDS

TEST THE TEST

A sea urchin has five sharp teeth in its mouth that it uses to scrape algae off of rocks. If you find a test on the beach, try shaking it. The rattle you hear is the sound of the broken teeth inside.

Sea urchin test

SAND DOLLARS

Notice the five-pointed star on the back of a sand dollar's test. It is a reminder that this animal is related to the sea star too.

Sand dollar test

When it's alive, a sand dollar is covered with a thick, velvety fuzz of short spines. The sand dollar uses these spines to pass food along its body to its mouth.

When the water is calm, sand dollars stand up on their sides, stuck in the sand. When waters are rough, they lie flat and bury themselves.

Live sand dollars

FIELD FACT Are you thinking this animal doesn't look anything like a dollar bill? You're right. It is named for a silver dollar coin, which used to be much more common.

ANIMALS

SEA BISCUIT

Live Sea biscuit

A sea biscuit looks a lot like a sand dollar, but it is puffier. It is shaped like the top of a muffin. A sea biscuit will sometimes decorate itself with pieces of shell and seaweed as added protection from predators.

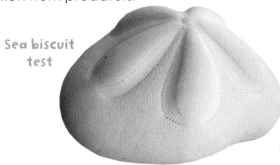
Sea biscuit test

55

Sea Stars

Bat star with sea urchins

People often call sea stars starfish, but they are not fish. Sea stars are echinoderms.

At first glance, a sea star looks like it has only arms. But looks can fool you: Turn it over and you'll see hundreds of little wormy things wriggling about. These are the sea star's feet! Each of these "tube feet" ends in a sucker that helps the sea star move and hold on extra tight to rocks and shells.

A sea star's mouth is hidden right in the middle of the forest of tube feet. Its arms are called rays, and any one of them can take the lead. Each ray has an eye spot at its tip. Sea stars can't see shapes, but they are sensitive to light.

It is okay to gently pick them out of the water for a short time for a closer look, but put them back as soon as possible.

Northern sea stars

FIELD FACT If a sea star loses an arm, it will grow another one. As long as a portion of the central part of the body is attached to it, a single sea star arm can grow into a whole new sea star!

The mouth of a sea star

Four-armed sea star

Sunflower star

Most sea stars have five rays, but the **sunflower star** adds rays as it ages. It can have as many as 24 rays and grow as large as two feet across.

Northern sea stars and **common sea stars** are found all over the East Coast. They range in color from yellowish to brown to purple. **Ochre sea stars,** which are usually purple or orange, are common on the Pacific coast. There are a lot of **bat stars,** which have webbing between their rays, in central California.

Dried-out common sea star

SEA STAR SLURPEE

When it's hungry, a sea star will climb onto some unlucky shellfish like a clam or oyster and wrap its strong arms around the shell. It pulls and pulls, and as the shells slowly come apart, the sea star pops its stomach out of its mouth and into the mollusk. Once inside, the stomach turns its victim into soup and slurps it up. When the meal is over, the sea star sucks its stomach in again and moves on.

Ochre sea star

Sponges

Live finger sponge

For a very long time, people couldn't decide whether sponges were plants or animals. It's easy to see why they were confused! Now we know that sponges are some of the very oldest animals on Earth. They've been around for 600 million years!

Can you see how this sponge got its nickname?

Sponges live their whole lives underwater attached to something hard like a rock or a shell, but pieces often wash ashore after a big storm. Underwater, a **finger sponge** looks like a plant. The broken-off branches you find on the beach, though, are skinny and long, giving this sponge the creepy nickname dead man's fingers.

When you look at a sponge under a magnifier, you see that it's covered with

MIRACLE WORKER

Many sea animals can grow new body parts when they're hurt, but sponges are the absolute champions! Even when a sponge is squeezed through a strainer and broken up into the tiniest bits, it can rebuild itself within just a few days!

holes: some small, some large. Sponges trap microscopic food particles floating in the water as the water flows through their body. Water is sucked in through the small holes, and sponges shoot waste out of the large holes. A large sponge can circulate 400 gallons of water a day!

The **boring sponge** secretes an acid that burns holes in mollusk shells. If you find a clamshell covered with tiny holes, that's a sure sign of a boring-sponge attack.

Boring sponge washed up on the beach

Shell damaged by a boring sponge

Bread crumb sponges crumble like stale bread in your hands, but you might not want to handle them at all: They're stinky!

Live bread crumb sponge

Red beard sponges look like bright-red plants underwater. You may find them on the beach.

Red beard sponge on the beach

Live red beard sponge

Jellyfish

A jellyfish isn't a fish, and it's not made out of jelly! A jellyfish

Sea nettles

is mostly water, yet it is one of the most successful hunters in the sea.

Trailing its long tentacles like bright scarves, a jellyfish almost seems to be dancing as it swims through the water. But don't be fooled: Those tentacles are dangerous. They're covered with tiny poison-tipped darts called nematocysts (*nem*-a-tuh-sistz) that are triggered to shoot anything they touch. Nematocysts are like

Sea nettle

capsules, each with a coiled thread inside that is lined with barbs. When the jellyfish comes into contact with anything hard—a fish, a human—the thread uncoils and shoots poison into the offender. A jellyfish uses its tentacles to paralyze prey. If you run into one, you might get an itchy sting.

Sea nettles are common jellyfish in the Atlantic and Pacific Oceans. There are different species of sea nettles, but all of them have powerful tentacles covered with nematocysts. Using their nematocysts, sea nettles are able to kill fish that are larger than they are.

Moon jelly on the beach

Moon jellies are perhaps the world's most common jellyfish. Clear and roundish, they're not really able to control their motion, so they mostly just drift with the current. Although

Moon jellies

they use their tentacles to sting tiny fish and other prey, their stingers aren't strong enough to penetrate our skin. If you happen to brush up against a moon jelly, you might get a small rash, but nothing more serious.

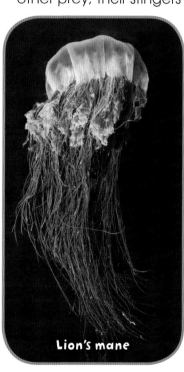

Lion's mane

The **lion's mane** is the largest of all jellyfish. Its tentacles can be more than 100 feet long! Lion's manes often wash up on beaches.

ANIMALS

DON'T TOUCH!
When it's washed up on the beach, a jellyfish looks like a blob of goo, but beware: Even when it's dead, a jellyfish can sting you.

Jellyfish Look-Alikes

The **Portuguese man-of-war** looks like a jellyfish, but it's actually a colony of many tiny animals living together. With its purplish "sail"

Portuguese man-of-war

floating on top of the water, it's easier to spot than most jellyfish. Stay clear of this critter, because its sting is especially painful.

By-the-wind sailor

The **by-the-wind sailor** is also a colony of animals. Its sting doesn't hurt people. It can't swim. Instead, it uses its small clear sail to drift across the sea, traveling whichever way the wind blows. Hundreds of them can wash up on the shore after a storm.

GOOD NIGHT, BEACH

At night, with all the daytime beachgoers gone, you can hear the sounds of the seashore even better.

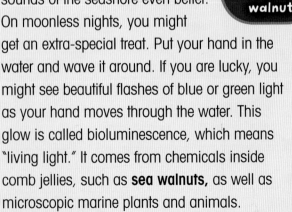

Sea walnut

On moonless nights, you might get an extra-special treat. Put your hand in the water and wave it around. If you are lucky, you might see beautiful flashes of blue or green light as your hand moves through the water. This glow is called bioluminescence, which means "living light." It comes from chemicals inside comb jellies, such as **sea walnuts,** as well as microscopic marine plants and animals.

FIELD FACT Christopher Columbus saw bioluminescence for the first time when he came to the New World. He said he saw "candles moving in the sea."

Comb jellies, like the sea walnut and sea gooseberry, may also look like little jellyfish, but they are not. They don't have stingers. Look closely and you can see the eight rows of tiny fluttering hairs propelling them through the water.

Comb jelly

Comb jelly on the beach

MAKE IT

HEY, GOOD LOOKIN'!
Want a better look at what's going on in a tide pool or shallow cove? Here's how to make yourself a handy underwater viewer.

You'll need:
- **A large can—a coffee can is best—with ends removed by a grown-up**
- **Plastic wrap**
- **A large, thick rubber band**
- **Duct tape**

1. Stretch the plastic wrap tightly over one open end of the can. Wrap the rubber band around it. Make sure the plastic is smooth and flat.

2. Fasten the edge of the plastic wrap to the can with the duct tape to keep water out.

3. Put the plastic-wrapped end of the can into the water, and look through the open end.

ANIMALS

63

Tunicates and Bryozoans

There are some things you come across in your beachcombing that are completely puzzling. Is it an animal? A plant? *Alien vomit?*

DISAPPEARING BACKBONES

At birth, **tunicates** look like tadpoles. Each one has a simple eye, a tail, and gills. They even

Different types of sea pork, washed up on the beach

have a simple backbone called a notochord. But before long, the free-swimming youngsters attach themselves headfirst to a hard surface like a rock, a shell, or the bottom of a boat. They lose all their tadpoley parts. Some, like the **sea pork,** end up looking a lot like a wad of chewing gum.

A tunicate called a **sea squirt** is covered by a leathery bubble that has two holes on top. It traps floating food particles by sucking water in one hole and spurting it out the other. You can see a

Sea squirts are sometimes called sea grapes. Can you see why?

sea squirt squirt for yourself by gently squeezing the bubble. It's like a natural water pistol.

Sea squirt on the beach

Sea squirt

PLANT LOOKALIKES

One example of a **bryozoan** is **sea lace.** It is like a busy apartment house. If you look closely under a magnifier, you will see that the crust is made up of hundreds of itty-bitty shelled compartments. Behind each "door" lives a tiny animal called a zooid.

Sea lace

Lettuce bryozoan

Because they look so much like plants, bryozoans are also called moss animals. Some bryozoans, like the **lettuce bryozoan,** look like wilted lettuce. Others, like

Spaghetti bryozoan

the **spaghetti bryozoan,** remind people of soggy noodles. The **tufted bryozoan** resembles a fern plant, but it is really made up of flattened shell-like tubes, each containing a little zooid.

OPEN UP!

NATURE FINDS

If you find a piece of seaweed covered in bryozoans, place it in a jar of seawater and watch it for a while. You might see the tiny doors open and close as zooids stick out their tentacles and sweep the water for food.

Tufted bryozoan

Insects and Spiders

You've probably already met a few of the insects that live at the beach. Some are colorful, some are hard to spot, and some are really annoying!

Dragonfly

WHAT'S ALL THE BUZZ ABOUT?

A **dragonfly,** hovering like a helicopter, is fun to watch. One of the fastest insects anywhere, it can zip along at speeds of 60 miles per hour.

Dragonflies have been around for 200 million years. Prehistoric dragonflies were huge, with a wingspan of two and a half feet!

FIELD FACT Long ago, people were superstitious about dragonflies because of their odd looks. Some folks were afraid to spend the night outside, because they thought dragonflies would sew their eyes together while they slept!

Unless you can stop breathing, you can't hide from a **mosquito.** They are attracted to the carbon dioxide in your breath. Every time you exhale, they can smell it—up to 60 feet away. Here's a surprise: mosquitoes don't suck your blood to eat. They actually live on plant nectar. Only the female mosquito bites, and she does it because she needs the protein and iron in your blood for her eggs to grow. Mosquitoes bite some people more than others, depending on how much they like the smell of someone's sweat.

Mosquito

Even worse than a mosquito bite is the razor-sharp bite of the female **deerfly.** The **greenhead fly** is the deerfly most commonly found at the beach—look out for it!

Greenhead fly

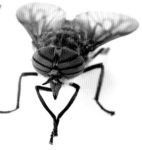

BOLD CRITTERS

The bold colors on the wings of a **monarch butterfly** are actually a warning that this insect is poisonous. It's as if the butterfly is waving a brightly colored flag that says "I taste yucky! You'll get sick if you eat me! Go find someone else for dinner!"

Monarch butterfly

Wolf Spider

The **wolf spider** lives in a hole in the sand. Unlike most spiders, it doesn't spin a web to catch its food. It chases its prey, hunting it like a wolf (though not in a pack)!

ANIMALS

Wolf spider

A Squirmy, Wormy World

Hidden under the sand, there is another bustling world to explore at the beach. Take your shovel at low tide and dig down a bit. You may uncover some very wriggly creatures.

Clam worms

Many people use **clam worms** as bait when they go fishing. The clam worm has a bright-blue line down its underside. Many pairs of dark-colored bristles help it move. During the day, clam worms burrow in the sand, but at night, they come out to hunt.

Bloodworms

Bloodworms are also used for bait, and look a lot like clam worms, but they are purplish pink. Watch out! Both clam worms and bloodworms have sharp pinching claws that can give you a nasty nip.

Bloodworm

Milky ribbon worms are usually cream-colored or pink. They grow up to four feet long. If pick you it up, it may fall apart into many pieces. Don't freak out, you didn't kill it: Each broken piece will grow into another worm!

Milky ribbon worms

There are some worms you hardly ever see, but the signs of them are all around you

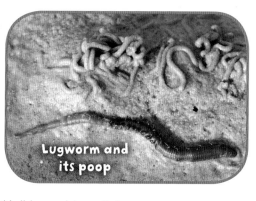

Lugworm and its poop

at the beach. Walking at low tide, you may see small coiled piles of sand by your feet. That's worm poop! **Lugworms** live under the sand in the bottom of U-shaped tubes. When a lugworm is hungry, it crawls up to the surface through one exit hole and swallows sand. It digests tiny food particles in the sand. Later it backs up to the other exit hole and poops out the leftover sand in these tidy little curled ropes.

The **trumpet worm** is also called the ice cream cone worm. Using sand and sticky mucus, the worm builds itself a tapered tube to live in that looks just like an ice cream cone. Even though they're only a single grain thick, these cones are very sturdy. Some survive long after the worm has died.

Trumpet worm and its tube

ANIMALS

EXAMINE THE GRAINS

NATURE FINDS You can sometimes find these little "ice cream cones" lying in the sand. If you do spot one, examine it under a magnifier: You will see what a skilled builder this worm is. The grains in the cone are fitted together as neatly as bricks in a chimney.

Animal Tracking

Bird tracks

A sandy beach is a great place for finding animal tracks.

NIGHTTIME ACTIVITY

Even animals you never see during the day, like mice, raccoons, and foxes, may visit the beach in the darkness of night. No matter how secretive they try to be, though, you can probably follow their footsteps in the sand.

FOLLOWING THE TRAIL!

Your best bet is to look early in the morning before the sand has been disturbed by human beachgoers—after a hard rain is best.

If you find a good set of tracks, take a photo or draw a sketch of what they look like. See how far you can follow the tracks—you might be surprised where they lead you.

At low tide, it's fun to follow the winding trail of a **mud snail.** Snails may be known as slowpokes, but these critters really book! They plow through the wet sand like a bloodhound, tracking the scent of some dead animal.

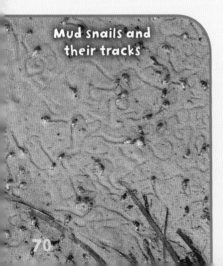

Mud snails and their tracks

Sea turtle tracks

If you spot raccoon tracks, you will see that some of them are longer and more triangle-shaped and others are shorter with more defined grooves. The longer prints are the hind feet. The shorter prints are the front feet.

Gulls, Skimmers, and Terns

When you think about the beach, you probably picture seagulls circling the water, and can even hear their distinct cries in your mind.

Herring gull

An adult **herring gull** has a white head and a soft, gray back. It can live to be more than 30 years old. Year-old gulls are the same size as their parents, but their feathers are spotty brown.

You may see a gull fluttering above the beach, dropping a clam onto the rocks again and again. It's trying to break open the shell and get to the tasty meat inside—if another gull doesn't steal it away first! If a herring gull strolls close enough, you might see a bright-red spot on the side of its beak. Gull chicks know that if they peck their mother right on that spot, she will start feeding them.

A **laughing gull's** black head and red beak make it easy to spot. Its loud and cheerful call—*ha, ha, ha!*—sounds like the gull just heard a really good joke.

Laughing gulls

The knife-sharp red bill of the **black skimmer** is strange: The lower half is longer than the top. Skimmers fly low, dragging their

Black Skimmer

lower beaks in the water, hoping to scoop up something good to eat.

Tern

Many kinds of **terns** have black heads too, but their sharp beaks and narrow, pointed wings make them easy to tell apart from laughing gulls and skimmers. You can often see terns hunting for fish near the beach. They flutter above the water until they see something good, then fold up their wings and dive!

BEWARE OF MAMA TERNS

Terns lay their eggs right in the sand. If you get too close to a nest, look out! Terns may be small, but they are fearless if they think you're going to hurt their babies. They'll dive-bomb you, peck your head, and even poop on you!

A tern in flight

Herons and Egrets

With their graceful, long, S-shaped necks, herons and egrets are beautiful birds that are easy to recognize.

When you see a **great blue heron** fly overhead, you might think you are seeing a pterodactyl. With a wingspan of six feet, the great blue heron is the largest heron in the United States. Its feathers are

Great blue heron

a soft blue-gray. You can often see the birds wading in shallow water on their stiltlike legs. When hunting, a heron will stand as still as a statue. It watches the water, waiting for fish, reptiles, or even small mammals to swim by. When some unsuspecting prey gets close enough, the heron will strike in a flash, using its sharp beak like a spear.

Great blue heron

FIELD FACT Great blue herons are large, but they do not weigh very much—only five or six pounds. Like all birds, they have hollow bones, which keep them light.

Great egret

Great egrets may be solitary hunters, but when it's time to breed they gather in large groups called colonies. The males and females build their nests together, and take turns caring for their young.

Great egret

Snowy egret

The **snowy egret** has a dramatic crown of feathers on its head.

ENDANGERED HATS

Years ago, women liked to wear hats decorated with feathers from egrets and other birds. Thousands of birds were killed for their feathers. The demand was so great that snowy egrets and many other kinds of birds were almost wiped out. Luckily, people realized that the birds were much more important than the hats. Just in the nick of time, laws were passed to protect these beautiful birds from being hunted to extinction.

Birds of Prey

Unlike many birds of prey, ospreys and bald eagles live by the water. It's a thrill when you see these mighty birds soaring overhead.

Osprey

OSPREY

The underside of an osprey is white or mottled. The feathers on its back are dark brown. Its eyes are bright yellow.

Because of their diet, ospreys are also called fish hawks. They hunt their prey in spectacular dives from as high as 200 feet above the water. You can tell an osprey has spotted something when you see it hovering in one spot. Then, all of a sudden, the bird will fold its wings and plummet into the water with a big splash, attacking with its clawed feet.

Ospreys usually nest on the top of dead trees or power line poles near the water. In some places, people have built special platforms for ospreys' huge nests, which can weigh up to 1,000 pounds.

If you see an osprey flying above you, listen for its soft little chirp: *cheep, cheep!* It's not the sound you expect to hear from such a big, powerful bird.

Osprey nest

Bald eagle

BALD EAGLE

A bald eagle isn't really bald. Its head is covered with brilliant white feathers. Not that long ago, eagles were a rare sight, but now it's possible to see them soaring overhead along many U.S. shores.

Eagles have excellent eyesight. They can see an animal as small as a rabbit or mouse moving a mile away.

A bald eagle is one of the strongest birds in the world. One was recorded carrying a 15-pound fawn! Females are larger than males, with a wingspan almost eight feet wide. Bald eagles mate for life, and return to the same nest year after year.

ANIMALS

COMEBACK KIDS

Because of pesticide poisoning, eagles and ospreys were in danger of disappearing from the planet forever. We are lucky that people in the 1960s and 1970s realized what a terrible thing that would be, and took action to ban certain pesticides and protect these grand birds. Now ospreys and bald eagles are making a comeback.

Waterbirds

Although ducks and geese don't live at the seashore all the time, many kinds visit the beach at different times of the year.

You can often see flocks of ducks floating just beyond the waves. In many species, the males and the females look different. Some ducks will dive deep in the water to get their food. Others dabble: They dip their heads down and flip their bottoms up to grab something good just beneath the surface.

Male eider

Female eider

DIVERS

Eiders are the largest ducks on our shores. The bright-white, black, and greenish (on the neck) feathers of the male eider make it easy to spot, even from a distance. Female eiders are brown.

Eiders dive all the way to the seafloor for prey, including sea urchins. People have long used their down feathers as the stuffing in blankets, pillows, and jackets.

The **red-breasted merganser** has a long, thin bill and a cool hairdo. It looks like a rock star!

Male red-breasted merganser

Female red-breasted merganser

Common loons are known for their wild call. They live most of their lives in the water, and

Common loon

only come to dry land to mate and hatch their eggs. Their legs are far back on their body, which is great for swimming but rotten for walking.

DABBLERS

Look for duck butts tipping up and down in the water—**mallards** are everywhere! They are the most common ducks in North America.

Male mallard

Female mallard

Mute Swan

ANIMALS

Mute swans are originally from Asia. They were brought here as living decorations for parks and estates. Some escaped captivity, and now the birds are found in many coastal areas. Although they are quite beautiful, they are also aggressive, so keep your distance.

Brants are small black-headed geese about the size of ducks. They spend their entire lives near the coast, and have a special gland that allows them to drink salt water.

Brant

Shorebirds

Have you ever played at the edge of the surf, trying to get as

Shorebirds looking for food

close as you can without getting wet? Racing in and out with every wave? It's so much fun! Many shorebirds appear to spend their days playing the same game. But they're not goofing around. They're looking for food.

STAYING SAFE AT THE SHORE'S EDGE

All this scurrying about is serious business. These shorebirds don't have webbed feet like ducks, and they don't know how to swim. As they skitter along the edge of the surf, they have to be careful not to get knocked over by a big wave.

These birds are so small and fast-moving that it's often hard to tell most of them apart. But here are a few of the cast of characters you might meet on the beach.

killdeer

A **killdeer** has brown wings and two black rings on its neck and chest. If it thinks its chicks are in danger, a killdeer will try to distract the predator by pretending it has an injured wing.

The beaches where **piping plovers** hatch are often restricted from human activities during nesting season to give these delicate little birds a better chance of survival. A plover chick is so tiny it looks like a piece of popcorn

Piping plover in summer

Piping plover in winter

stuck on two little toothpick legs.

During the spring and summer, piping plovers have a black band on their chest and an orange bill. In the winter, the black bands fade and the bill becomes black.

American oystercatcher

American oystercatchers and **sandpipers** use their long bills to poke at the wet sand looking for food.

Sandpiper

Beach Relics

As you walk along the beach, scan the sand for other things that animals may have left behind.

FEATHERS

Birds use feathers for lots of different things. They use them to keep warm and dry, or to attract a mate. And of course, birds use feathers to fly. Feathers have different shapes depending on the job they do.

- The softest, fluffiest feathers are called **down.** Down feathers keep birds warm by trapping air close to their bodies. Blankets and jackets filled with down keep people cozy too!

Down feather

- If a feather has a stemlike shaft, or quill, running down the middle, it is probably a **contour feather.** These feathers cover a bird's body. They are usually more colorful at the tip than at the base.

Contour feather

- Is the quill of your feather off to one side? This is a **flight feather.** These are the feathers on the outer edge of the wing that help the bird fly.

Flight feather

BONES

A heavy bird would have trouble flying. That's why birds' bones are lighter than those of most animals. In fact, most bird bones are hollow. A bird's feathers weigh more than its skeleton!

Bird skull

When they fish, birds such as gannets and pelicans crash headfirst into the water. Why don't they crack their skulls? They have air sacs in their skulls that work like a car's air bags to absorb the blow. If you find a bird skull on the beach, look for large hollow spaces in it where the air sacs would have been.

TEETH

Most of the shark teeth you find on the beach are fossils from sharks that lived long ago. Sharks have been on the planet for 400 million years. When they die, their bodies may decay, but their teeth sink to the bottom of the ocean, where they get covered in sand and mud. Over many, many years, these turn into fossils.

Shark teeth fossils

Millions of shark teeth wash up on beaches all around the world every year.

ANIMALS

MERMAID'S PURSES

"Mermaid's purse" is the nickname for the egg case of a shark or its relative, the skate. Usually when you find them on the beach, they are empty, but every so often you can find a case with a single unhatched shark or skate embryo inside.

Mermaid's purses

Pelicans, Cormorants, and Anhingas

These birds are often seen sitting on rocks, jetties, or wharves. It's always fun to watch them fish.

White pelican

PELICANS

With a big, stretchy pouch hanging from its long beak, there's no mistaking a pelican! Look at the sky and you may see flocks of pelicans flying just above the water, stretched out in a long, single-file line.

There are two kinds of pelicans along our shores, and it's easy to tell them apart. **White pelicans** feed while swimming, scooping up food in their large bills.

Brown pelican

Brown pelicans fly above the water, searching for fish. When they spot something good, they make a loopy dive and grab a pouchful of water and food. Watch them bend their heads down to drain out the water and then tilt their bills up to gobble up the fish.

FIELD FACT A pelican can carry three gallons of water in its pouch—three times more than its stomach can hold.

Brown pelican

CORMORANTS

Cormorants are graceful, long-necked birds with glossy black

Cormorant

feathers. They are excellent hunters. To chase down a tasty fish, they can dive 100 feet.

FIELD FACT Cormorants are so good at catching fish that in Asia, some fishermen use the birds to fish for them. They attach a leash to the cormorant and put a collar around its neck that's too tight to let the bird swallow what it catches. When the cormorant grabs a fish, the fisherman pulls the bird in and takes the fish for himself.

ANHINGAS

An **anhinga** looks a lot like a cormorant, but it has silvery patches on its wings. The heads of the females are lighter than those of the males. It spears fish with its long, sharp bill. Sometimes, a fish will get stuck

Female anhinga

ANIMALS

Male anhinga

on an anhinga's beak, and it has to pry the fish off with a tree limb or rock.

FIELD FACT The anhinga has a couple of funny nicknames. It is called water-turkey because of its long tail and snake-bird for its habit of swimming with its long neck just out of water.

BASKING IN THE SUN

Cormorants and anhingas lack the oil glands most seabirds have for waterproofing their feathers. You will often see them sitting on a rock or buoy, wings outstretched, drying themselves.

Seabirds

There are birds that live almost their whole lives out at sea. We only get to see them when they hunt for fish near the shore, or during the short time they come to dry land to lay their eggs.

Northern gannet

The **northern gannet** is a striking white bird with black wingtips, a yellowish head, and a broad, strong bill. Seeing a flock of gannets feeding on a school of fish is a thrilling sight. The birds plunge into the water, each dive ending in a splash.

With its big, fat, multicolored bill, the **puffin** is known as a sea parrot or the clown of the sea, and a group of puffins is called a circus. They only come to land to raise their chicks, nesting in burrows on rocky cliffs.

Puffins

GREEDY GRABBERS

Puffins eat small fish, like herrings and sand eels. They chase their prey down by flying underwater, using their wings to swim. A puffin's festive beak unhinges, dropping down and allowing it to carry a lot of fish at one time—the record puffin mouthful is 62 sand eels!

Puffin

With its long, black wings and forked tail, a **magnificent frigatebird** looks like Batman, but acts like a pirate, attacking other birds in flight to make them spit out their food. Then, in a flash, the frigatebird swoops down, catching the stolen booty in its beak before it can land in the water. Males have a bright-scarlet throat pouch that inflates like a balloon during mating season. Females have a white breast.

ANIMALS

Female magnificent frigatebird

Male magnificent frigatebirds

Migrations

Leatherback turtle

Many of the animals you see at the shore are only passing through on their way to other places far, far away. Every year, traveling along the same routes their ancestors have followed for generations, millions of animals set out on great voyages called migrations. They go in search of food or warm weather or safe places to raise their young.

Gray whales have the longest migration of any mammal in the world, traveling more than 12,000 miles every year. They spend the summer feeding in the rich, cold waters of the Arctic. Come fall, pregnant females swim all the way down the Pacific coast to Mexico, where they give birth to their calves in warm, protected lagoons. In the spring, the mothers and their young pass close to the California coast as they head back up north. (For more on whales, see pages 92–93.)

Gray whale

Leatherback turtles have the longest migrations of any reptile. Females travel more than 3,000 miles to their nesting grounds.

Leatherback turtles

Monarch butterflies have an amazing migration too. These delicate insects make their way from the United States to Mexico, traveling up to 3,000 miles. How do they know where to go? No one knows. Their young are

Migrating monarch butterflies

born in Mexico, and it is only their children's grandchildren that return north. Somehow they are born knowing the way. Some of these little guys even return to the very same tree their ancestors lived in.

Terns

Terns are the champion travelers of the entire animal world. Some Arctic terns make a round-trip voyage of more than 22,000 miles every year. They live in an endless summer by flying pole to pole. They breed up north, and when the days start getting shorter, they head down to Antarctica. Over its lifetime, an arctic tern will have covered enough miles to make it to the moon and back!

ANIMALS

Marine Mammals

Harbor seal

Mammals need air to breathe, which makes it pretty hard for them to live full-time in the ocean, like fish do. In spite of the challenges, there are some mammals that do live in the sea. Some of them live their whole lives away from land, but others visit the seashore, where we can get a good look at them.

SEA OTTERS

Along the coast of California, you can see

Sea otter

otters swimming in the kelp forests just offshore. Otters like floating on their backs best. They will sleep that way, and mama otters cradle their babies on their bellies while nursing.

Looking like lazy, saltwater couch potatoes, otters even snack on their backs! A hungry otter will put a rock on its belly and smash a clam or mussel against it until the shell breaks and it can get to the yummy meat inside.

Unlike most marine mammals, sea otters don't have a layer of fat to insulate them in cold water. Instead, they have a beautiful coat of thick fur that traps air close to their bodies, keeping them warm. Years ago, they were hunted nearly to extinction for their fur. Now that hunting them is illegal, their numbers are coming back.

Sea lion

SEA LIONS

Sea lions can rotate their strong rear flippers forward, allowing them to "walk" on land. The trained animals you see in aquariums are usually **California sea lions.** They are very social animals: You can often see big groups of them on the beach or rocks, or floating offshore.

Gray Seal

SEALS

Sea lions have an external ear flap, where most seals do not. As its numbers grow, the **gray seal** is becoming an ever more common sight on East Coast beaches. Males are dark brown, while females are tan. Gray seals will eat almost anything they find—even birds, if they can catch them. Although they share the same waters, you can

Harbor Seal

tell a **harbor seal** from a gray seal because a harbor seal is smaller and has a face like a puppy!

ANIMALS

THE SEAL DANCE

Seals may seem as curious about you as you are about them. A seal swimming near shore may suddenly pop its head out of the water and give you a long, hard look. If you catch a seal spying on you, say hello and wave. If it's still looking, pick up a stick and pretend that you're casting out with a great big fishing pole. Seals sometimes gather to see whether you've hooked any good fish for them to eat.

Whales

North Atlantic right whale

Most of the time, you have to travel out into the ocean to see these enormous marine mammals. But there are places along our coastlines where—at the right time of year—you can see these magnificent animals from the beach. It's a very special treat.

Gray whale

Whales travel close to both coasts at different times during the year. (For more information on whale migrations, see page 88.) If you want to whale-watch without getting on a boat, you may catch a glimpse of **gray whales** off the Pacific coast in the spring, when they travel close to the shore.

Fin whales, also called finbacks, are the second-largest animals in the world (after blue whales), averaging about 60 feet in length. Fin whales can be seen from the Atlantic coast.

Fin whale

Humpback whale

During the summer, you can see giant **humpback whales**—more than 50 feet long—from the beaches of Cape Cod, Massachusetts. A humpback is black on top, with a fin in the middle of its back. Its underside will have a unique black-and-white patten. They jump clear

Humpback whale

out of the water, raising their enormous tails high in the air before diving back in. Between spring and fall, humpbacks can also be spotted off the coast of Maine and elsewhere in New England, as well as off Long Island.

In the winter, endangered **North Atlantic right whales,** along with fin whales and humpback

North Atlantic right whale

whales, can be seen off the Virginia coast.

FIELD FACT Whales have been spotted in busy harbors such as New York and Boston in recent years. New laws require cargo vessels in these areas to slow down, in order to protect the North Atlantic right whale.

LOOK—AND LISTEN!
On a quiet foggy day when the water is as still as glass, you may hear a low *whoosh* as a whale offshore slowly exhales a deep breath. That is a sound you will never, ever forget.

Dolphins

Thanks to their smiling faces, dolphins are easily the most popular marine mammals. Dolphins are also thought to be very intelligent.

Dolphin mother and child

Dolphins live in tight family groups called pods. If one member of a pod is injured, the rest will often try to rescue it.

Dolphins' eyesight and sense of smell aren't very good, but they are still excellent hunters. They depend on their hearing, using a form of sonar called echolocation. Dolphins make sounds that travel through the water and bump into fish. The dolphins listen to the returning echoes to determine where the food is.

CHATTY, CHATTY DOLPHINS

If you could listen underwater when a dolphin pod is near, you would hear a symphony of clicks, squeaks, and whistles. Every member of the pod has its own identifying whistle.

Bottlenose dolphin

DOLPHIN SPOTTING

Orca

Most people only see dolphins in marine theme parks, but in the Pacific Northwest, it's possible to see one kind of dolphin simply by standing on the shore. Although they are often called killer whales, **orcas** are actually huge dolphins. A male orca can grow to be nearly 30 feet long. The dorsal fin (that's the one on its back) of the male can be six feet tall. In the same way that detectives use fingerprints to identify people, naturalists can recognize individual orcas by markings on their dorsal fins and back.

Most orcas live their entire lives in pods. Members of the same pod talk to each other in their own special language.

Bottlenose dolphins are the dolphins most commonly seen from the beach. These dark gray animals are widespread along our coasts. They often come very close to shore. Adults can be 8 to 12 feet long, and can weigh as much as 1,500 pounds. The curve of a bottlenose dolphin's mouth makes it look like it is smiling all the time.

ANIMALS

Bottlenose dolphin

Sea Turtles

Sea turtles are ocean animals. The only time we get a glimpse of their lives is when they arrive on our beaches to lay their eggs.

Green turtle

A sea turtle egg buried in the sand

Throughout the spring and summer, female sea turtles come ashore on beaches from Virginia to the Gulf of Mexico. They crawl up past the high-tide line and dig holes in the soft sand with their rear flippers. After neatly burying the eggs, the mama turtles head back to the ocean, never seeing their babies.

Several weeks later, the eggs are ready to hatch. The babies emerge only at night. Scientists believe that newborn turtles need to see the moon and stars clearly to find their way to the sea.

Green turtle nesting

Years later, the females return to the exact beach where they were born to lay their own eggs.

Kemp's ridley turtle hatchlings

Kemp's ridley turtle

Loggerhead turtle hatchlings

Loggerhead turtle

The males live the rest of their lives at sea, never returning to dry land. There are many types of sea turtles, including **green turtles, Kemp's ridley turtles, loggerheads,** and **leatherbacks.**

There is only one other time you might come across a sea turtle on the beach. Sea turtles live in warm water, but sometimes young ones get thrown off course into northern waters. In the fall, when water temperatures cool, a wayward turtle gets "cold-stunned": Its body temperature drops, and it may wash ashore when it gets too weak to swim. If you find a cold-stunned turtle on the beach, get help. It can be rescued and returned to warmer waters.

FIELD FACT The temperature of the sand the eggs are buried in determines what sex the hatchlings will be. If the sand is too warm, only females will hatch. Scientists worry that as temperatures rise around the world, fewer male turtles will be born.

Leatherback turtle

Plants and Algae

Anything that grows at the beach needs to be adapted to sandy soil—or no soil at all. Since algae do not have roots, they are not plants. But you'll often find these plantlike seaweeds washed up on the beach.

Because it's often windy at the beach, the grasses, shrubs, and trees that populate the coasts need to be able to withstand serious winds. And some of the plant life helps to protect the beach from erosion.

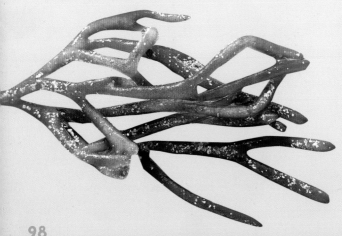

Seaweeds

Seaweeds live surrounded by water, so they don't need roots like land plants do. Many types of seaweed have something called a holdfast anchoring them to rocks or the seafloor with a strong natural glue.

Green algae

Large, leathery, brown ribbons of **kelp** sometimes wash up on the beach with the holdfast still attached to a rock.

Kelp

Green algae on rocks

Green algae on sand

Try not to ignore the most common seaweed at the beach—because if you do, you might end up on your bottom! At low tide, it's very easy to slip on wet rocks covered with a fine fur of **green algae.**

Off the California coast, **giant kelp** grows in thick underwater forests. Giant kelp is one of the fastest-growing living things on the planet. Growing at a rate of more than two feet a day, it can reach a length of 150 feet or more in just a few months.

Giant kelp

Sea lettuce

Sea lettuce on the beach

A seaweed's color depends on how deep in the water it grows. The deeper the water, the darker the seaweed. Light-green **sea lettuce** lives near the surface. Dark-red **dulse** grows in deeper water.

Dulse

BEACH HAIR

MAKE IT

Look for rocks with seaweed attached. Don't they look like heads with funky hair styles? Collect a few and line them up, then draw or paint on faces for your own creative mermaid gallery.

Pop It! Eat It!

Not all seaweeds are alike. When you inspect a pile of seaweed on the beach, you may come across ones with neat little air bladders. You may also find types of seaweeds that show up on restaurant menus!

Bladder wrack

Dried bladder wrack

Bladder wrack on the beach

NATURE'S BUBBLE WRAP

Some seaweeds, like **bladder wrack** or **knotted wrack,** are studded with gas-filled bumps. These help the seaweed float closer to the water's surface, allowing it to soak up precious sunlight. If you find a piece on the beach, try squeezing these little bubbles between your fingers. Pop!

FIELD FACT Many people refer to both bladder wrack and knotted wrack as rockweed.

Knotted wrack

Knotted wrack

YUM!

After a big storm, you can find lots of seaweed washed up on the beach. Look at a piece under a magnifier. You'll probably discover some little hitchhiking creatures that make seaweed their home.

Fried dulse

Many marine animals like to eat seaweed. People do too. It is packed with vitamins! Sea lettuce is made into soup in Japan. People fry **dulse** into crispy chips, but you can also eat it raw. Seaweed is even found in ice cream, chocolate milk, and toothpaste! Look for *carrageenan* on the ingredients label: It's made from **Irish moss,** a red seaweed you can find in dense clumps at low tide.

Most of the seaweed that washes up on the beach doesn't taste very good at all, so if you want to try it out, you're better off getting it from a market or restaurant.

Irish moss

Plant Superheroes

With everything else to see and do at the beach, it's very easy to overlook the simple grassy plants scattered around. But they are important—they help keep the beach healthy and strong.

EELGRASS

Even though **eelgrass** grows in salt water, it's not a seaweed. You find eelgrass in calm coves and bays. An eelgrass bed is a special neighborhood. Lots of sea animals use these underwater forests for food and protection. They provide a safe place for fish to lay their eggs and for the young to hide out in. And birds—particularly ducks and geese—eat tons of eelgrass.

An eelgrass bed is a great place to explore at low tide. With a viewer (see page 63), you can see lots of cool animals darting around—sea horses, pipefish, scallops, crabs, and shrimp.

When you're checking out an eelgrass bed, be aware of the incoming tide. The water can come back in faster than you expect!

Eelgrass

Beach grass

BEACH GRASS

Beach grass is another unsung hero of the seashore. It helps build up beaches. All the individual blades of beach grass you see growing out of the sand are connected underground by a thick mat of roots. The roots act like a net, trapping and holding down sand that would otherwise blow away in the wind.

Even though they're right next to the ocean, the sand dunes where beach grass grows are a lot like a desert. Freshwater disappears quickly, escaping between the grains of sand. Beach grass makes the most of every rainstorm, taking in as much water as it can by opening up its blades wide. When the weather is hot and dry, the blades roll up tight to keep moisture in.

Don't walk on beach grass. It can withstand a lot, but not your footsteps.

FIELD FACT Beach grass is also called compass grass, because when the wind blows a grass blade over, its sharp tip traces a semicircle in the sand. Like a weather vane, it shows you which way the breeze is blowing.

PLANTS AND ALGAE

It's Not Easy Being Green...

The seashore is a hard place for a plant to live. In the winter, wild winds blow and salt spray burns. In the summer, the sun blazes down on open sand. And freshwater is almost as scarce on the beach as it is in the desert. Plants need to be tough to live by the sea!

Sea rocket

Just like a cactus in the desert, beach plants like **sea rocket** and **seabeach sandwort** (or seaside sandplant) have thick rubbery leaves that can hold water.

Seabeach sandwort

Most seaside plants grow low to the ground to keep out of the punishing winds. **Dusty miller** is a short, pale-green plant that is covered with white, wooly hairs that help insulate it from the heat and cold.

Dusty miller

In spite of the challenges, seaside plants still manage to grow beautiful flowers and yummy fruits and berries. **Salt spray rose,** originally

Salt spray rose

from Asia, bursts with bright flowers during the summertime. It also bears tomato-like fruit called rose hips. You can eat them raw, although they are pretty tart. People cook them into sweet jelly. They are full of vitamin C.

Beach plum

Beach plum is another delicious fruit you can find at the beach. (Do not eat anything you find on a walk without the permission of a grown-up!)

Bayberries

You can't eat **bayberries,** but people use them to make scented candles. **Cranberries,** on the other hand, are delicious at Thanksgiving!

Cranberries

Other pretty plants include **beach pea** and **sea lavender.**

Beach pea

Sea lavender

Seaside trees

Pitch pine

Trees are a rare
sight at the beach.
The hot sun,
salt spray, and
constant winds make it difficult for
them to grow up tall and mighty.

Shore pine

Scrub oak

Trees that do manage to grow at the beach, like **pitch pine, shore pine** and **scrub oak,** are often stunted versions of their inland relatives. The **Monterey cypress,** which grows on the rocky cliffs of California, is so bent over and twisted from battling the Pacific winds that it often looks like a gnarled ancient man. These trees are some of the oldest in the world.

Monterey cypress

There are some trees that grow straight and tall by the seashore: **palm trees.** Palm trees are probably originally from Malaysia, but now they're found all over the world because their giant seeds, coconuts, can float across oceans. Palm trees can get so tall because they have deep, powerful roots that anchor them in the ground, keeping them from falling over when strong winds blow. **Royal palms** and **coconut palms** are two common types of palm trees.

Royal Palm

Mangroves are found in the warm-water swamplands of Florida. Mangroves are the only trees that actually grow in salt water, and they have many unusual features to help them survive such a challenging setting. They have special roots that absorb oxygen from the air, and they get rid of the excess salt through tiny holes in their leaves. Mangroves anchor themselves in the mud by shooting out hundreds of curved roots, creating an underwater maze that

Coconut palm

Mangrove roots

many sea animals like to hide in for protection.

The dense network of roots also traps mud, building up the seashore and protecting the coastline from the destructive force of hurricanes.

Mangrove

PHOTO CREDITS

HAPPY BEACHCOMBING!

The best beachcombing spots are often the calm shores of bays and coves where great big waves aren't crashing onto the sand all the time. And when it comes to beachcombing, it pays to be an early bird. If you can get out there in the morning before the sand has been trampled by other people's footsteps, you might find something that would be buried later in the day.

Visit the same beach often to learn about its natural rhythms. Every time you go back, the shore will be different in some way. You will discover something new every time.